Snake Bite

by David Clayton

Illustrated by Jolyon Webb

Chapter 1

Dead Wolf Point

Tim and his dad had climbed for four days. Above, the great hills bit the sky like sharks' teeth. They were black spikes in a sky as red as fire. Now, the great plain lay like a brown carpet below them. Tim and his dad were way above the world and alone, so alone.

That night, they camped at Dead Wolf Point. The name made Tim shiver. His dad laughed and checked the map as he sat by the camp fire. Tim's dad always checked everything. He was like that. He was a policeman. The trouble was, he also checked up on Tim a lot. Tim wasn't happy about that. It always made him feel like a little kid.

"Tomorrow, we're going up Snake River Canyon," Dad said for the tenth time. "Then after that it's up and up to Indian's Peak. Takes me back to when I was as old as you."

Tim knew *all about* Snake River Canyon. Tim knew *all about* Dad and his trip. He could not forget it. He heard tales like this every day. If the tales weren't about hunting, they were about fishing. If they weren't about fishing, they were about adventure.

"I know," said Tim, "you told me …"

"Don't you *want* to be here, Tim?" His dad's face was a little darker, a little redder.

"Of course I do, Dad," Tim lied. Then he sat quietly, eating a plate of hot beans.

Summer slipped away fast up here. Some days the air was warm. Tonight, the wolves huddled in the chill. Tim was thinking about his best friend, Jim. Tonight Jim would be playing basketball down the street. All the gang would be there: Tony, Sam, Pete. Tonight they would be having fun.

Up in the mountains, it was like being on another planet. Tim was used to Coldwater Bay with its wide lawns and white wooden houses. The wildest thing there was Mrs Martini's dog. It always tried to bite him when he delivered her paper.

This place was so wild that it scared Tim. He had never camped before. But, of course, he could not tell his dad what he really thought.

The beans were lovely. They warmed Tim's tongue. They made his throat glow. He could feel his body getting warmer by the second. It was a great feeling.

Now night was coming fast. High above, a jet unzipped the orange sky. Tim could feel his mind flying east with it.

"You're quiet," said his dad.

"I'm thinking, just thinking," said Tim.

Sometimes he thought that his dad would like to check on his mind too.

Far below, Tim could see lights way across the great darkness. Maybe it was Fort Laramie or Mule Creek? The great world was quiet, so very quiet. Above, the million clear stars made you feel so small. Suddenly, Tim felt cold inside. Suddenly, he was glad that his dad was with him in this lonely world.

"Time for bed," said his dad. The great pines above them had started to swish like a mighty sea. A few moments before, the air had been dead calm.

"Weather's changing, son," said Tim's dad. "It's always like this in the mountains. We've had it clear all the way up here. *Now* it changes. Good night."

Tim slipped deep into his sleeping bag. He was tired and yet he couldn't nod off. It was time to talk to Charlie.

CHAPTER 2

Talking to Charlie

Tim peeped out of his tent. His dad was asleep in his bag on the other side of the fire. No tent for Dad. He was hard. But, anyway, he *was* asleep.

Tim popped his head back in again and removed Charlie from his pack. Tim had got Charlie for Christmas when he was five. Charlie was a soldier in a green and brown uniform. He only had one leg.

Every night, Tim talked to him. Sometimes there was nobody else to tell things to. Of course, Charlie never said anything back, but he never shouted, either. Tim liked Charlie.

Of course, Dad would laugh and laugh if he knew that *his son* had a doll to talk to. However, Tim didn't care. Charlie listened to him a lot more than his dad did.

"Hey, Charlie, do you think that this trip will be the end of all the Rambo stuff?"

Tim could tell that Charlie didn't think so.

"No, me neither. I wonder what would put him off this sort of thing for good?"

Charlie said nothing.

"You're right," said Tim. "Who knows?"

Tim could hear the wind singing in the trees. He saw the flap of the tent and the flicker of the fire. Then he tucked Charlie into his sleeping bag.

"Sleep on it, Charlie. I'll talk to you again tomorrow."

Soon, Tim was asleep.

The next morning, the smell of breakfast woke Tim. He did not jump out of his cosy sleeping bag though.

"Come on, son. Chow!" Dad always knew when it was time to eat.

Tim stepped out into the cool, bright sun. The wind had dropped but there were clouds way over to the west. He washed his face in an icy stream. That woke him up.

Next camp was way up on the mountain.

"That's where you get to be a man," his dad had said.

Tim looked up at the great peaks. That's where you could get to be *dead*, he thought.

CHAPTER 3

Snake River

It was nearly six. Dad wanted to be in the canyon by seven.

There were no trees or wolves or bears in the canyon. Just huge red cliffs cut into a deep crack by the icy, green Snake River. Far away, Tim hadn't been impressed. Right there, he gasped when he saw the great walls of rock.

Everywhere there were boulders as big as houses. It made Tim feel very small. It was like walking into the mouth of a crocodile. And it was getting quite hot. Five hours of walking and Tim's legs were worn out. Tim's dad flopped down. He was worn out too.

"Didn't remember how tough it was," Dad gasped, opening his pack. "Some slopes!"

Lunch was nothing special, cheese, bread and water. As he ate it, Tim looked about him. Here, the walls were just cliffs. There were no side canyons. He was about to say something when he saw his dad's eyes look upwards. Tim's dad had stopped mid-bite. He was staring hard upstream.

"What's up, Dad?" Tim was puzzled.

"**Trouble!** Pack up, now. **Move!**"

Tim's dad had lost his tiredness. He was moving fast. Tim looked at the sky. A black layer of cloud was running fast across the V-shaped cut of the canyon way up ahead.

"What's up, Dad?"

"Mountain storm. **Bad news!**"

"So?"

"This is Dead Man's Corner, the narrowest part of the canyon."

"But the storm's way over there. Miles away."

"And where do you think all that water will go?"

Tim jumped up. As he did, Charlie
fell on to a rock. Tim didn't see him
in the rush.

"Down *this* river!" Tim gasped.

By the time they had packed up, the
canyon had fallen into shadow. Clouds
were racing across the sun. Far away, there
was a dull 'boom'.

"How long have we got?"

"Long enough, I hope, or else God help
us!" Dad's voice was jumpy now.

"How high does the water get?" asked
Tim as they scrambled downstream,
towards a wider part of the canyon.

"Well," said his dad, "it moves stones
like that."

The rock he pointed to was bigger than
a truck.

Now they were half-walking, half-running. The walls were still steep. Tim and his dad were gasping and groaning, sweating and grunting. Rocks loomed up ahead. If only they could just get to them. If only ...

Then it happened. Tim's dad slipped
and fell ten metres down a glassy boulder.
CRACK! It was an awful sound, bone on
stone. But Dad never even stopped. His
arm was hurt but his pack had saved his
back. He yelled, "COME ON!"

Now, the rain hit them like nails as the dark cloud swept over.

A few hundred metres away, they heard the RUMM-RUMM-RA-RUMM! of the flood as it raced like a great express train down the canyon.

Quickly Tim and his dad climbed to a spike of rock twenty metres up. Then Tim tied loops of rope around himself and his dad. Dad's right arm was useless. Without the rope they would be washed away.

RA-**RUMMMMM!!!!!!** The thunder of white water came closer and closer and closer.

"HOLD ON! HOLD ON!" croaked Dad.

SHHHH!!!!!!!! The water came, ripping and pulling them. It threw them about like dolls.

Then *under* they went.

For two seconds, three seconds, five, ten, they were in a swirling, twirling darkness. Then down, down, down went the water. The canyon crashed and thundered. Lightning sparked backwards and forwards above as the storm swept over them.

For ages they could not move, but the rope had held.

"OK, Tim?"

"Yes. You?"

"Same," his dad lied. His face was grey.

Soon, the air grew lighter and warmer. Within an hour, the sun was warm as ever and the fat Snake River slid below their feet.

Carefully, carefully, they limped down the gorge. When they were clear, they tried the radio. It was dead.

By midnight, they made it back to Dead Wolf Point.

"It's ... ah ... only a five-hour walk ... to the Ranger camp south of here," said Dad. His arm looked bad. "We'll make it by morning."

"No, Dad," said Tim. "I'll run there now."

"No ... no."

"YES, Dad!" he could hardly believe his ears. He could see the surprise in his dad's eyes. "But, first, I'll make you a fire."

Soon, the fire was drying them out. Soon, a brew of hot coffee was on the boil.

"We didn't climb Indian's Peak, did we, Dad?" said Tim.

"No, but we beat the Snake at Dead Man's Corner and not many people live to say that."

Tim stood ready to go. He looked about him. The lights twinkled far out across the plain. High above, the stars looked down on the great zig-zag canyon. His father huddled close by the fire.

"I've got to tell you something, son," Dad said. "Me and my dad never did climb Indian's Peak. It was all a dream. Just my dream. My dad never took me anywhere."

Tim took his compass and torch out of his wet pack. Then he noticed that Charlie was gone. As he lined up the compass with the Ranger camp, he thought about the day. His mind was full of the great red canyon, the black sky and the green Snake. Then there was the accident. Then him helping his dad to survive. And, finally, the reason why Dad had brought him up here in the first place.

"Take care, Dad!"

"And you, son ... thanks!"

As Tim jogged away into the darkness, the Snake hissed by, ready to bite again some day.

A few minutes later, Tim's dad picked Charlie out of *his* pack.

"Maybe Tim doesn't need you any more, Charlie," he said. Then he smiled and sat Charlie by the fire to wait with him.

Martin's Midnight Muddle

IMPACT TEEN LIFE, SET A

Martin is always in a muddle.
So perhaps it's not a great idea to
go on a camping trip with him!

Hey, Lads,
I've Just Had a Great Idea!

IMPACT HUMOUR, SET A

When Wayne has a great idea,
it's time to get out of the way!

You're No Dog, Marmalade!

IMPACT HUMOUR, SET A

David wants a dog. Any old dog with a wet nose and a leg on each corner will do. David gets his wish when a huge orange and white striped dog arrives. But Marmalade isn't just any old dog.